This igloo book belongs to:

....

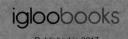

Published in 2017
by Igloo Books Ltd
Cottage Farm
Sywell
NN6 0BJ
www.igloobooks.com

Illustrated by Paul Nicholls
Original story by Linda Staten

Cover designed by Nicholas Gage
Interiors designed by Helen Jones
Edited by Stephanie Moss

STA002 0617
2 4 6 8 10 9 7 5 3
ISBN 978-1-78557-737-6

Printed and manufactured in China

Twinkle, Twinkle, Little Star

igloobooks

Twinkle, twinkle, little star,
how I wonder what you are!
Up above the world so high,
like a diamond in the sky.

When the sun has gone to bed,
stars light up the sky instead,
shining all their starlight down,
watching over all the town.

Near the water, wide and deep,
little seal pups, half asleep,
start to close their weary eyes
underneath the starry skies.

Little rabbits, soft and grey,
burrow down at the end of the day,
snuggling up all warm and tight,
while the starlight twinkles bright.

Cuddled up without a peep,
baby birds have gone to sleep,
while a soft and gentle light
keeps them safe throughout the night.

Once the day has come and gone,
tired kittens meow and yawn.
While they sleep, the cheerful beams
light their little kitty dreams.

Up above, that twinkly star
shines on down to where you are.
Close your eyes and rest your head.
Snuggle up all warm in bed.

It's time to sleep. The day is done.
Goodnight, sleep tight, my little one.

Twinkle, twinkle, little star,
how I wonder what you are!

Up above the world so high,
like a diamond in the sky.